Mary Woodward

Old rhymes for old friends

Mary Woodward

Old rhymes for old friends

ISBN/EAN: 9783337265052

Printed in Europe, USA, Canada, Australia, Japan

Cover: Foto ©Andreas Hilbeck / pixelio.de

More available books at **www.hansebooks.com**

OLD RHYMES

FOR

OLD FRIENDS.

BY

MARY ANNA WOODWARD.

Printed for Private Distribution.

CAMBRIDGE:
PRESS OF JOHN WILSON AND SON.
1874.

CONTENTS.

OLD RHYMES FOR OLD FRIENDS.

JANUARY 1, 1860.

ANOTHER year has anchor cast
   In dull oblivion's tideless bay ;
Gone, with the dim wrecks of the past,
   From the proud realm of day.
Another changeful year is fled
To the still mansions of the dead.

Wild notes of wail are on the air,
   And Northern spirits hurry by ;
OLD WINTER shakes his frosty hair
   Beneath an angry sky ;
And ice-isles, with a grinding sound,
Break on the shores that ocean bound.

What changes have swept over earth
   Since the departed year was born !
Fires have gone out on many a hearth,
   And many hearts forlorn
Been crushed beneath the weight of woes,
While worms have fed on beauty's rose.

Grief has outstretched the faded form
   Of many a loved one on the bier;
Hope fled, a wanderer in the storm,
   Like old distracted Lear;
And Peace beheld a serpent cold
Twine round her dove's soft neck its fold.

Love has thrown by the bridal veil
   And draped her wings in funereal black;
While Memory, with visage pale,
   On perished joy looks back,
Like Marius 'mid ruins, lo!
Ambition sits in voiceless woe.

Another poor frail ship of time
   Moors, with furl'd canvas, by the shore, —
Her freight not worth an idle rhyme,
   Her stormy cruising o'er;
While a new bark is speeding fast,
Gay colors streaming from her mast.

On to thy haven, voyager bold,
   Regardless of the hidden reef;
Filled, in thy wide, capacious hold,
   With things of joy and grief.
Together there lie snugly stored
Both cradle-couch and coffin board.

Ere Eighteen Hundred Fifty-Nine
   In wintry darkness closed its flight,

HUMBOLDT, proud learning's mighty chief,
  Withdrew from life and light, —
An earthquake's roar from slumber dread
Could not awake the mighty dead.

And a thick cloud of funereal gloom
  May well, New England, cover thee;
For MANN, within his Western tomb,
  Sleeps far from his native sea.
His voice no more shall learning's hall,
Or Senate, startle with its call.

The Icebergs, from their caverns deep,
  The tidings sad proclaim,
That in their cold embrace they keep
  The hero sought by Kane.
Conjecture's voice is ever hushed,
The hopes of LADY FRANKLIN crushed.

Virginia, from her mountain crest,
  Sends forth a melancholy moan
For BROWN, the martyr of the West,
  The hero, overthrown.
His eye is darkened with eclipse,
Hushed are his noble Spartan lips.

List! plaintive notes come floating up
  From Hudson's " Sunny-Side : "
Our pride, our loved and honor'd one,
  Our IRVING, too, has died —

But lives! If genius dwells on high,
Exalted worth can never die.

Thus pass away the wise and great,
   Thus fall the valiant and the brave;
For mortals in their best estate
   Are bubbles on the wave:
So was it in the days of yore,
So will it be for evermore.

A CALL TO THE CALICO PARTY.

WILL you come to the Calico Party,
  All ye who are daintily fed?
Will you come to the calico party?
  For Kansas is crying for bread.

Ye fathers, and mothers, and sisters,
  Lay your broadcloth and satins aside,
And the laces, and trimmings, and fixings,
  That so lately bedecked the young bride.

When your storeroom is crowded with plenty,
  And want never squints at your door,
Your breakfast steams hot on the table, —
  Then's the time to remember the poor.

The fields have not whitened with harvest,
  The toil of the reaper was vain ;
While the cry has gone daily to Heaven, —
  "O God, give us rain, give us rain."

When your silks and your satins are faded,
  And your broadcloth consumed by the fly,
You will find your old calico dresses
  Stored safe in a wardrobe on high.

Then come to the calico party, —
   We promise a plain bill of fare, —
Oh! don't send the hackney'd regret,
   That indeed you have nothing to wear.

JANUARY, 1856.

ONE year ago we dedicated then
Our annual offering to the fast young men ;
An unexpected change has crossed our dream,
And fast young women seems to be the theme.
Not fast of foot, for rare does lady good
Soil her light gaiter by a thing so rude.
Not long ago the lady walked to balls, —
Now calls a coach to give her neighbor calls ;
Not long ago the daughter in her prime
Helped her old mother down the tide of time.
Now the old mother when her best is done
Scarce keeps her daughter till meridian sun.
Should nature spare such imbeciles, for what
From morn till night to thrum the piano forte.
Oh, much I fear my warning is too late,
And some are doomed to meet the fig-tree's fate.
The mother's motto was a thrifty home,
The daughter's motto is a sugar-plum.
See them march up like troop of grenadiers,
Bold front, bare-headed, and uncovered ears.
Don't be alarmed, for modesty don't fear, —
A fifteen-dollar bonnet in the rear,
For such they call it ; but, the truth to tell,
Jockey, or cap, or flower-pot, just as well.

Our mothers had a dress-up suit for Sunday,
Who never heard of a brocade on Monday.
But Tuesday, Wednesday, Thursday, all the week,
Brocade and Satin promenade the street!
O luckless wight who has a wife like these,
Do lay by something for the sheriff's fees, —
He will be paid, the inexorable man, —
Say to the rest, just catch me if you can.
The party invitation reads at seven.
The vulgar, only, go before eleven.
And then the dress, what lacks 'bout neck and ears
Is amply made up in the full arrears.
The entertainment too, oh! who will dare
To sketch the outlines of their bill of fare?
Old folks to name the viands must import
A *cuisine* from Napoleon's kitchen court,
Make the new cider of their father plain
By transmigration into old champagne.
Economy, that household word once dear,
Shocks the refinement of the lady's ear;
And Dr. Franklin, should he chance preside
O'er the arrangements of a modern bride,
Would get a cuff, — oh, yes, and get a flout,
And bid with his old maxims to get out,
You, and old fogies of your clan, may clear.
Spirit of Brummell, make arrangements here!
The home-made wives, and many such we know,
Who to their husbands keep through weal and woe,
Are now displaced by California widows, —
Whose marriage contract sells to highest bidders,

Throw off their husbands with the *nonchalance*
Of country partners, in a contra dance.
Old ladies now are bid to step aside,
And clear the track for yester's flaunting bride.
I'll tell you what, make much of such you have,
A few short years will land them in the grave ;
And from the present feeble, pampered race,
None will come up to fill the " old woman's " place.
Should such a monster in my country then,
As an old woman of threescore and ten,
Astound the world, the news will fly,
On telegraphic wings from sky to sky ;
From future Barnum, or some greater rogue,
The veriest show, in all his catalogue.
I speak in sorrow, and I will be brief,
Nor wish to invade the shades of private grief,
Of when few friends around the dying-bed
With sympathy arrayed our holy dead.
In place of simple robe we now import
The latest fashions from thy mart, New York,
Perverted taste to robe the mouldering form
In the same vestments as the bridal morn.
A modern funeral, see the broadcloth coat,
The nodding plume, and the grief-bordered note,
To tell the world that six months we must mourn,
Then gilding, house repairing, all are done,
To oil the gearing of great Fashion's car,
That it may run more swiftly than before.

·   ·   ·   ·   ·   ·   ·   ·   ·

CODE OF MANNERS.

THE writer asks to be informed,
　　By youth or man or sage,
What code of manners are extant
　　In this enlightened age.

The curious questions daily asked,
　　Unconscionably free,
Would once have sent the author forth
　　From " good society."

A few examples I will give,
　　From out the very many ;
Do answer, graduates from High Schools,
　　What's done in this dilemma?

And first they ask, " What is your age?
　　You've past the sentimental,
And must remember well the days
　　Known as the Continental."

When they a toothless matron meet,
　　Regardless of her frown,
" Where did you get your ivory,
　　Of Dr. North or Brown?

" And then your hair, that once was gray,
   Is now so very brown ;
Give me the rule for coloring,
   And I'll inform the town.

" And then your teeth and colored hair,
   They look so very ' funny,'
They would pay well, e'en if they cost
   John Jacob Astor's money.

" And who gets up your morning meal,
   And who prepares your tea ?
And do you dine at noon, I ask,
   Or not till after three ?

" And who may be your laúndress now,
   And who repairs your clothes ?
Not many pieces in a week, —
   For so the story goes.

" And tell me then, there is no harm,
   What does your living cost ?
It cannot be so much, I'm sure,
   As boarding with ' mine host.'

" And did you buy that magic stuff,
   By Mrs. Humbug sold ?
' Twill take the wrinkles from your brow,
   Your locks will shine like gold.

"No matter if you're sixty, dear !
  ' Tis all the same I ween ;
Before to-morrow's sun comes up,
  You'll be but sweet sixteen.

"Now tell me what your bonnet cost,
  And what's the price of fur,
And did you buy of Mr. L.
  Or buy at Rochester ?

"Then what's the sum you paid, I ask ? —
  Don't quibble at the price, —
I've got a catalogue of all
  The furs considered nice.

" There's Mrs. A. paid twenty-five,
  And Mrs. B. paid thirty,
And Mrs. C. paid thirty-five,
  And Mrs. D.'s were forty.

" But this is common stuff, you see,
  Fit only for *poor* men ;
For all the ladies that I know
  Have paid their ten times ten."

Now they can wear their muffs and cuffs,
  And never see the harm ;
And round their heads can twist about
  A pound or two of yarn.

And they can wear a cape and cloak,
  And all the set complete,
And never feel too warm, although
  It's eighty, Fahrenheit.

But should you chance to walk the street
  With two or three warm shawls,
Although 'tis zero, " What a fudge ! "
  The fur-clad lady bawls.

We have a grand society,
  " Excelsior " is its name,
Where all our wisdom, talent, wit,
  On Friday night convene.

There mimic plays and comic sports
  All gratis can be seen,
But would not something practical
  Be well to intervene.

As once a week they meet to roam
  Imagination's field,
I would suggest that once a month
  They read Lord Chesterfield.

Although in all our modern shops
  The work is obsolete,
You'll find it, in an antique form,
  At Stevens', Market Street.

A moral here you plain can see,
  Without old Argus' eyes,
'Twould save a power of quibbling
  And scores of stale " white lies."

AN APOLOGY.

Poet nor rhymester by descent,
  Or from Parnassus' hill,
I sometimes send a moral forth
  In simple doggerel.

One day in solitary muse,
  A fancy sketch I drew, —
All personality and pique
  Were absent from my view.

But poor Philanthropy, at best,
  However well designed,
Does not a glad response obtain
  From every generous mind.

The fashions once I dared attack, —
  That hydra-headed thing, —
Where rich and poor and age and sex
  Meet on one levelling.

And, like Pandora, from her box
  She showers promiscuous ills,
As milliners and merchants show
  By long protested bills.

The Doctors next I criticised
  (We numbered then sixteen),
But when I met them on the walk
  They always looked serene.

And when the cows my grounds invade
  I wished them all in glory,
With not a candle to light up
  Their way to Purgatory.

The Pope well knew this libel came
  From the great Yankee nation,
But ne'er has thundered from his throne
  An excommunication.

Presumptous grown, we then approach
  The printer's easy chair,
And there inscribe the wicked name
  He dooms his boy to bear.

And yet the printer never winced,
  Nor did the bills disclaim ;
I would that, when the garment fits,
  We all might do the same.

But when you touched the gossips !   Ah,
  It surely was " no go," —
With sneer and flout the word went out
  It was " supremely low."

Cowper once wrote a pretty piece
  About a little mouse ;
And Burns descended *lower* still,
  And wrote about a louse.

How can we celebrate the birth
  Of such a vulgar man,
Who dares a lady's bonnet charge
  With vagrants on the brim.

All pardon here I humbly ask,
  All wrong would disabuse,
And seek more genial subjects hence
  For my uncultured muse.

ON THE DEATH OF LOUEE.

[The boarders at the Palmyra Hotel were grieved to hear
of the death of their favorite Mocking-bird. The following
lines, written for amusement, are worthy of being dressed up
in type. We hope not to offend the author by publishing
" her crude thoughts " without authority.]

COME, Andrew, Kate, and Lyman, all,
And raise your wail within the hall,
The minstrel's dead, oh, sad to say!
His lay was closed on Sabbath day.
The cypress-wreath, Louise, entwine,
And let not music, mirth, or wine
Profane the hour; but let the tear
Join the lament o'er Louee's bier.
Three years ago, one pleasant day,
While journeying in the month of May,
A stickler for the rule of right,
'Gainst slavery ready for a fight,
Unmindful what the South might say,
Kidnapped and brought you far away,
From Southern home, and nestlings dear,
And trees that blossom all the year.
'Tis true we nursed with tender care
A bird so sweet, with songs so rare;

But still you longed for orange flowers,
For myrtle boughs and jasmine bowers.
When with caresses round we'd linger,
In high disdain you'd peck the finger,
And teach, by your revengeful mouth,
A slave's a slave, both North and South.
To find a name we long did tarry,
And conned o'er Tom and Dick and Harry ;
Then judging, from his mien elate,
He'd be an honor to his State,
" Louisiana," all too long,
" Louee," for short, was fixed upon.
May Lawyer P. your praise rehearse,
In classic prose and plaintive verse,
And teach all warblers, far and near,
The mocking-bird's the bird of cheer.
For all who die beneath the sun,
Some will rejoice and some will mourn :
While we deplore with song and sigh,
Shanghais will wave their heads on high,
And bless their stars that death degrades
One who so long was " death on eggs."

TO MY OLD SHAWL.

I LOOKED on thee with pride, Old Shawl,
  When I was young and bold,
And thought thy only province was
  Protection from the cold.

Life then was new to us, Old Shawl,
  And we without a plan ;
And I little thought thy history'd be
  Analogous to man.

Thou wert the fashion then, Old Shawl,
  And with an honest pride
Thou met the high pretensions
  Of a January bride.

And to the party gay, Old Shawl,
  Thou clothed the fair young belle,
And thy sombre hue did not disgrace
  The passing funeral knell.

And many a heedless traveller,
  O'ercome by autumn's cold,
Has found a refuge from the storm
  Beneath thy ample fold.

And when the early frost has come,
 With its sly and subtle power,
Thy fleecy robe has lent its aid
 To guard the tender flower.

Thou hast acted well thy part, Old Shawl,
 In all the scenes of life :
Thou hast guarded well the Infant,
 Daughter, Father, Husband, Wife.

And now the felon in despair,
 As on the rail-car flies,
His hand-cuffs, emblems of disgrace,
 Protects from curious eyes.

This moral now thy life may teach :
 However good the past,
Let none presume, — we all may come
 To some base use at last.

A TRIBUTE TO MRS. MARY HEMINGWAY,

WHO DIED AT PALMYRA, FEB. 21, 1861, AGED 61 YEARS.

A STRANGER from the pilgrim land,
　　In simple habit drest,
I sought what then appeared to me
　　The very far, far West.

No letters-patent did I bring
　　Of wealth or high degree,
And was surprised to find e'en here
　　An Aristocracy.

Among the very few who sought
　　To know the lonely one
Was that dear friend whose genial worth
　　We all so deeply mourn.

And when New England's Holiday
　　Calls all her children home, —
Far distant from ancestral halls,
　　I'd none to bid me come.

She bade me to her ample board,
    With friends both kind and true,
While the young olives by her side
    Then numbered only two.

One of that little company
    Soon joined the angel band,
And that meek, gentle sister, too,
    Hailed for the Holy Land.

In after years when few choice friends
    Promised a mental feast,
My feet responded to the call
    To be an honored guest.

Through all the years of grief and pain
    That Heaven ordained her lot,
My ailments and my simple wants
    Have never been forgot.

Her friendship was no meteor flash,
    No ocean's ebb and flow ;
'Twas pure, sincere, and earnest too, —
    Unchanged in weal or woe.

Oh, may the mantle that she wove,
    And dropp'd in her flight above,
Descend on those who knew her best, —
    The daughters of her love.

TO THE BARD OF PALMYRA.

Who is this wondrous poet,
  The people all inquire,
That recently has risen,
  And set the world on fire?

Ah! proud would be our *Washington,*
  Thrice proud, did he but know:
It is an honored namesake,
  That's set the world aglow.

He is bereft of gratitude,
  Whose finger points with scorn
At this great and good philanthropist,
  That wrote the man of corn.

And glad must be the mother,
  That ever she was born
To rear so great a poet
  As wrote the man of corn.

And proud our common country,
  By rebels made forlorn,
To boast this trading genius
  That wrote the man of corn.

May future generations,
  And poets yet unborn,
Do homage to the hero
  That wrote the man of corn.

May all your great effusions
  Each library adorn,
Especially the masterpiece
  Known as the man of corn.

O persecuted poet!
  All jealous poets warn,
By lashing them severely,
  As you did the man of corn.

Lay on the lash, O poet!
  Till their proud spirits quail,
And they recant of saying
  You make your rhymes for sale.

Bard of Palmyra, you have placed
  High on the scroll of fame,
In living letters undefaced,
  A poet's honored name.

We are loath to have you leave us,
  But we must be resigned;
Some of your fine productions,
  In pity, leave behind.

Farewell, O shade of Byron!
Whose mantle surely fell,
And rests upon your shoulders, —
Palmyra *Bard*, farewell!

A TRIBUTE TO BETSEY LIVINGSTON.

[Oct. 4, 1855, Betsey Livingston, colored, twenty years a member of the family of W. P. Nottingham. Her remains were interred, with suitable solemnities, in his family enclosure, in our village cemetery.]

WHAT sadness fills our house to-day!
Have friends or kindred passed away?
Have any ties of love been riven?
Have half our hearts gone up to heaven?
Oh, no: an aged pilgrim gray
Of Afric's race has passed away.
Her fourscore years, how brief they seem
From Jordan's retrospective stream!
We will not on each merit dwell:
Her part she truly acted well.
Ladies to wealth and lineage born
Might of her true politeness learn;
With all respect to race and rule,
A lady of the olden school.
Deny the adage all who can,
'Tis true that " manners make the man."
The children round her fondly clung:
The law of kindness ruled her tongue.
A lofty turban, white as snow,
Adorned her venerable brow;

5

Her noble air and stately mien
Would well become proud Hayti's queen, —
For queen she was to all intent,
When on her household duties bent.
A floor so white, a taste refined
Might from its surface almost dined;
Tables like ivory all around,
With tempting viands richly crowned,
And lemon, pastry, lettuce, placed,
With taste peculiar to her race.
There virtues gave a moral tone
To all " the subjects round her throne."

A lonely traveller on my way,
I soon shall close my little day ;
Like her no kindred round my bier,
Strangers will drop the parting tear.
Our dear old friend has gone before,
But left behind the open door,
Through which we all shall pass so soon.
To that great feast where all find room,
Where bond and free surround the board
Spread for us by our common Lord.

A REMONSTRANCE.

O YOU wicked, wicked cows !
    Can't you find a place to browse ?
Will you over five bars leap,
    Like a nimble flock of sheep ?
Not contented with all that,
    Tray, Blanche, and Sweetheart, on your track ?
Without so much as asking pardon,
    Straight you scamper through the garden,
Then make the dirt and cabbage fly,
    And bid the mistress " mind her eye."
Then through the gate with one great dash,
    And down they come with such a crash,
The grand *dénouement* of your pranks,
    Like fashionable paper banks.
There's one particular old sinner,
    In every charge she is the winner:
I'll leave her not one ray of hope,
    But roast her like a pious Pope:
No " quarter " give to dying groans,
    But make cremation of her bones ;
And her own candles light her too,
    Where sinners get their passports through : —

A better thought, I'd save the light,
  To illumine some poor cot at night.
No doubt but she would scratch and scramble
  In Purgatory for a candle,
Or, if close cornered, she would seize,
  For her deliverance, Peter's keys.

FOR MY NEPHEW, JOHN LILLIE.

To declaim at School, at the Age of 11 Years, 1856.

Listen while a song I say
About the name of John to-day, —
A name so old and orthodox
Was sanctified by good John Knox;
John Calvin, too, we all revere,
Although his creed's somewhat severe;
And great John Milton, without sight,
Saw worlds of intellectual light.
Of all the kings on England's throne,
But one subscribed the name of John;
Our new born country, scarcely free,
Rejoices in the name of three:
John Adams, second President,
And John, " the old man eloquent,"
Then, by an accident, most rare
John Tyler took the chieftain's chair.
Van Buren had a princely son,
Now known as the apostate John;
Then old John Brown, the city crier,
And John Calhoun, the nullifier,
And John Fremont, the pioneer,
If beat by Jemmy, is his peer.

Long as our country's scroll shall stand,
John Hancock shows his noble hand;
When Sir John Franklin reached the pole,
He might have gone through Symmes's hole:
A frozen mummy he may choose;
I'd rather be a roasted goose.
When this great name became a hack,
'Twas metamorphosed into Jack.
Jack Tar, Jack Shepherd, and Jack Ketch,
Sailor, highwayman, hangman, each
Did some good service, one and all,
To keep in motion this great ball.
Jack Downing, too, the great ally
Of Hickory,* raised for him the cry:
The Ship of State would be a blank,
Without his foot on Biddle's bank.
Then there's that other dexterous son,
That nimble youth, Jack Robinson.
One Jack a giant did assault,
And one built up a house of malt;
The last of all came down the hill,
And broke his crown with little Gill.
This nickname, friends, does not belong
To Lillies, — they rejoice in John.
Don't think me arrogant, but free,
If I rehearse my pedigree.
In seventeen hundred fifty-three,
John Lillie first was lost at sea.

* General Jackson.

John Lillie second was his son,
And fought with our great Washington.
He died in eighteen hundred one,
And dropped his mantle on his son.
The fourth, just ceased to be a boy,
Lies on the plains of Illinois.
The fifth, your humble servant now,
Makes this his valedictory bow.

A REMEDY.

WHO all the horrors can unfold
Of a hard influenza cold?
The tongue, in cherry velvet drest,
Assumes a white fur-coat and vest;
And then such coughing, choking, sneezing,
Roasting, sweating, crying, freezing,
Such aching limbs, such ague shocks, —
'Twould seem Pandora and her box
Had been gulped down in one huge pill,
To make you heir of every ill.
And then the scores of remedies,
More painful far than the disease,
The pills and plasters, blisters, potions,
And little homœopathic notions,
From sixteen doctors, *all profound.*
.　　.　　.　　.　　.　　.　　.

Now take advice from simple wight,
And when you go to bed at night
Take a good draught of Adam's ale,
Of blankets plenty do not fail;
With a wet napkin on your chest,
And conscience clear, you'll go to rest.
The dogs the physic then may take,
Though sixteen doctors all should break.

LOTTIE LEE.

ONE day, last week, I took a walk,
    About the hour of five;
The children were just out of school, —
    The pavement seemed alive.

With cheerful face and nimble feet
    Came on the happy band;
I gave a look, — 'twas all, indeed,
    Familiar scenes demand.

At last a little girl of five,
    With careless step and air,
And eyes so bright, and curls so soft,
    Came dancing *solitaire.*

I stopped, and thought some Cuban belle
    Had sought our winter zone;
She could not be indigenous,
    So lovely, and unknown.

I asked her name; she stopped the chase,
    With voice and action free,
Then made her manners, and replied,
    " My name is LOTTIE LEE."

I've heard the chain of slavery clank,
  I've seen the auction block,
And all the vile machinery
  Which God's own image mock;

But never was my soul so sad,
  So dim my vision's ken,
As when upon that child I looked,
  And thought " it might have been."

I sought no grand cathedral's dome,
  No altar decked with gold,
But on that pavement cold and lone
  To Heaven my prayer I told.

How long, O God! I pray, how long
  Shall beauty such as this
Be doomed to toil for brother man,
  Or worse — for traitor's kiss?

O LOTTIE LEE! O LOTTIE LEE!
  Thank God, who gave you birth
Where Learning opens wide her doors
  To all the sons of earth.

Then walk erect, walk undismayed,
  Walk in thy birthright free;
No kidnapper shall dare invade
  The home of LOTTIE LEE.

'Fore such a wretch shall foothold get,
   For honor or for pay,
Niagara will turn his course,
   And run the other way.

The Empire State, all as one man,
   In Freedom's cause combined,
Would names and parties drive away,
   As chaff before the wind !

Your politicians, wrangling still
   If Kansas shall be free,
Come, read the answer in the face
   Of little LOTTIE LEE.

www.ingramcontent.com/pod-product-compliance
Lightning Source LLC
Chambersburg PA
CBHW030911260626
47169CB00008B/2801